by Lea Taddonio   illustrated by Mina Price

Head over Heels

First Dance

Spellbound

An Imprint of Magic Wagon
abdopublishing.com

To PB &J, my favorite combo —LT

For Mom & Dad —MP

abdopublishing.com

Published by Magic Wagon, a division of ABDO, PO Box 398166,
Minneapolis, Minnesota 55439. Copyright © 2017 by Abdo
Consulting Group, Inc. International copyrights reserved in all
countries. No part of this book may be reproduced in any form
without written permission from the publisher. Spellbound™ is a
trademark and logo of Magic Wagon.

Printed in the United States of America, North Mankato, Minnesota.
102016
012017

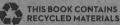 **THIS BOOK CONTAINS
RECYCLED MATERIALS**

Written by Lea Taddonio
Illustrated by Mina Price
Edited by Heidi M.D. Elston
Art Directed by Candice Keimig
Series lettering and graphics from iStockphoto

Publisher's Cataloging-in-Publication Data

Names: Taddonio, Lea, author. | Price, Mina, illustrator.
Title: First dance / by Lea Taddonio ; illustrated by Mina Price.
Description: Minneapolis, MN : Magic Wagon, 2017. | Series: Head over heels ; Book 1
Summary: Lola Jones does not think her big brother's best friend and basketball
  teammate C.J Kline knows she's alive, until one magical night at a high school dance
  changes everything.
Identifiers: LCCN 2016947655 | ISBN 9781624021923 (lib. bdg.) | ISBN 9781624022524
  (ebook) | ISBN 9781624022821 (Read-to-me ebook)
Subjects: LCSH: High school students--Juvenile fiction. | Best friends--Juvenile fiction. |
  Interpersonal relationships--Juvenile fiction. | Human behavior--Juvenile fiction.
Classification: DDC [Fic]--dc23
LC record available at http://lccn.loc.gov/2016947655

Table
of
Contents

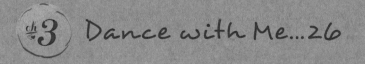
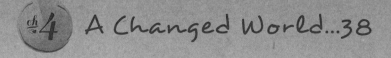

That One Boy

After school I wait for my best friend Kizzie at our usual spot. The hall is **CROWDED** and ***NOISY***. It seems like everyone at Washington High School is talking about the **dance** at the same time.

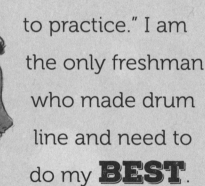

"Hey, girl!" Kizzie runs over with a big smile on her face. "I can't wait for tonight."

"I'm NOT going to the dance." I hold up my drumsticks. "I have to practice." I am the only freshman who made drum line and need to do my **BEST**.

Kizzie crosses her arms. "But the **whole** basketball team will be there."

"Who cares?" I roll my eyes. "If I even talk to a basketball player, Joseph gets **mad**." My big brother plays center for the Washington High **WARCATS**. They are the best team in the city.

Kizzie *sighs* and **PUSHES** her braids off her face. "This is a **problem** because C.J Kline will be there too."

"So what?" I try to ignore the *flutter* in the pit of my stomach. C.J Kline is the Warcats' star point guard and my brother's **BEST FRIEND**. He has black hair, brown eyes, and the kind of smile that makes you feel *good all over*.

"I heard C.J thinks you're **cute**."

"But he doesn't talk to me."

My *cheeks* feel **HOTTER** than fire.

"He never even looks at me."

Every girl has that one boy.
The one she has had a **crush** on
since **FOREVER**. C.J Kline is
that boy for me.

"Trust me, Lola. He does. You're just too **shy** to notice." Kizzie puts her arm around my shoulder. "Come out **tonight**. I know just what outfit you should wear."

OH NO. What have I gotten myself into?

The Secret Dance

My normal style is jeans and a T-shirt. Now I'm in the school gym in Kizzie's dress. It's **pink** and knee length, with an open back. I feel BARE.

"Don't worry," Kizzie says.
"That color makes you **POP**."

"I'm not worried," I mutter.

"Is that *right*?" Kizzie
puts a hand on her hip.
"You look like you want
to be somewhere else."

"Yes. I want to be
at **HOME** watching
movies or listening to
music."

"Look!" Kizzie **jumps** up and down. "The basketball team is here."

The Warcats strut into the gym like the **KINGS** of the school.

Everyone whispers and giggles, but who cares? The DJ has put on my song.

"Do you hear that?" I take Kizzie's hand. "Let's go *dance*." The beat is fast, and I feel the bass through my whole body. Music is my life. It is my **ESCAPE**.

When the song ends, I open my eyes and **FREEZE**. C.J is looking at me from across the room. I glance away. I look back. He glances over again. This is the *secret* dance we do. The one I don't tell **ANYONE** about.

Not my brother Joseph.

Not even Kizzie.

NO ONE knows.

C.J smiles and my heart

POUNDS because this time he

is not only looking. This time he

is *walking* in my direction.

ch 3

Dance with Me

"Hi, Lola," C.J says. The gym lights are low, but his smile lights up the **DARK**.

I like my name fine, but when he says it, I *love* it.

"Hey." I stare at my feet.

"You look like you're having

a good time. I saw you out

there *dancing*."

I **SHRUG** and brush my

hands over my skirt.

"Are you going to say

more than **one** word to

me?" he asks.

I *smile*. "Maybe."

His mouth turns up in

the corner. "*Dance* with me."

29

My stomach **drops**. "You know my brother won't like it."

My big brother has told me one hundred times **NEVER** to date any guy on his team. C.J is not just my brother's friend. He is his ***BEST FRIEND***.

"Hey! I got you to say more than one word." His voice is *teasing*. "And Joseph doesn't **SCARE** me."

The next song comes on. It is slow and **romantic**. Couples sway around us.

Kizzie stands behind C.J and **CLAPS** her hands.

"Okay, fine," I say. "I will dance with you. But don't say I didn't **WARN** you."

"You're worth the trouble," he says with a wink.

I don't have *butterflies* in my stomach. I have **dinosaurs** stomping around.

C.J pulls me close and puts his hands high on my back. He smells good, like **soap** and `aftershave`. He's breathing a little fast. Could he be as **nervous** as I am?

"What do you two think you're doing?" Someone asks in a **LOUD** voice.

I **FREEZE**.

It's Joseph.

A Changed World

"**WHAT** is going on here?" Joseph looks at both of us. "This isn't *cool*, Lola."

"Let me explain," I say.

"I asked your sister to **dance**. She said yes. **END** of story," C.J says.

"Yeah, you're right about that. This is the **END** of the story." Joseph GLARES at me. "Come on, C.J. Let's go." He marches over to his team.

I tap C.J on the arm. "Ever since Dad *left*, Joseph acts like he's the man of the house. He worries about Mama working too hard, about money, and about me."

"He doesn't have to worry about you." C.J touches my cheek. "You're funny, smart, and the **BEST** person on the whole drum line."

He cleares his throat. "You're *pretty*, too."

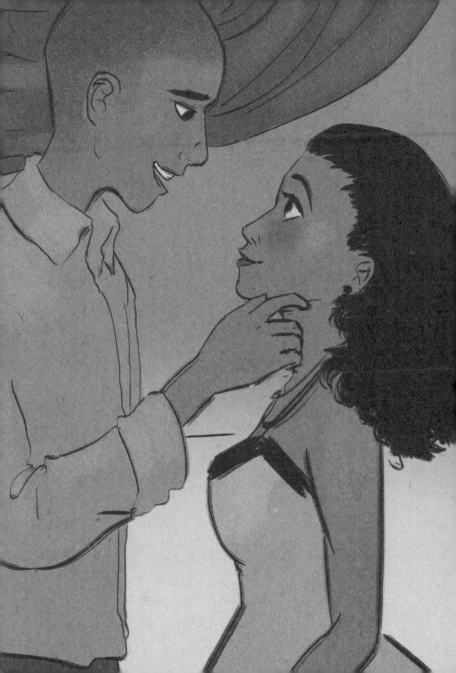

I **open** my mouth. No words come out.

"I'm not going to *disrespect* your brother. Remember, he's my brother too, and my teammate. But I want to *hang* out with you. You want to *hang* out with me."

"It's *impossible*," I say.

"You heard what Joseph said."

"I'm going to figure it out."

"It won't ever happen." I

ⓗⓤⓖ myself. "It's too hard."

"I don't mind a **CHALLENGE**.

Do you?"

"No. **But**... what if this doesn't work out?"

"What if it does?" He gives me a **wink** and walks away.

Everyone is **dancing** and laughing like nothing is different. But my **WORLD** just changed.